Axolotl

THINKS-A-LOTL SAYS CHEESE

by C.W. Estes
illustrated by Irene Saluzzi

PICTURE WINDOW BOOKS
a capstone imprint

Published by Picture Window Books, an imprint of Capstone
1710 Roe Crest Drive, North Mankato, Minnesota 56003
capstonepub.com

Copyright © 2025 by Capstone. All rights reserved. No part of this publication may be reproduced in whole or in part, or stored in a retrieval system, or transmitted in any form or by any means, electronic, mechanical, photocopying, recording, or otherwise, without written permission of the publisher.

Library of Congress Cataloging-in-Publication Data
Names: Estes, C. W., author. | Saluzzi, Irene, illustrator.
Title: Thinks-a-Lotl says cheese / by C.W. Estes ; illustrated by Irene Saluzzi.
Description: North Mankato, Minnesota : Picture Window Books, an imprint of Capstone, [2025]. | Series: Axolotls! | Audience term: Children | Audience: Ages 5-8. | Audience: Grades K-1. | Summary: Thinks-a-Lotl wonders if he can turn his smile upside down, but when the resulting frown freezes in place, he turns to his friends to help him restore his smile for picture day.
Identifiers: LCCN 2024020902 (print) | LCCN 2024020903 (ebook) | ISBN 9780756584467 (hardcover) | ISBN 9780756584429 (paperback) | ISBN 9780756584436 (pdf) | ISBN 9780756584498 (kindle edition) | ISBN 9780756584443 (epub)
Subjects: LCSH: Axolotls—Juvenile fiction. | Facial expression—Juvenile fiction. | Schools—Juvenile fiction. | Friendship—Juvenile fiction. | CYAC: Axolotls—Fiction. | Picture day—Fiction. | Amphibians—Fiction. | Facial expression—Fiction. | Schools—Fiction. | Friendship—Fiction.
Classification: LCC PZ7.1.E8523 Th 2025 (print) | LCC PZ7.1.E8523 (ebook) | DDC 813.6 [E]—dc23/eng/20240718
LC record available at https://lccn.loc.gov/2024020902
LC ebook record available at https://lccn.loc.gov/2024020903

Designed by Dina Her

Any additional websites and resources referenced in this book are not maintained, authorized, or sponsored by Capstone. All product and company names are trademarks™ or registered® trademarks of their respective holders.

TABLE OF CONTENTS

CHAPTER 1
WELCOME TO FROWN TOWN.......... 7

CHAPTER 2
TURNED UPSIDE DOWN............... 13

CHAPTER 3
SMILES FOR MILES.................... 19

Deep underwater lies the bubbly town of Sandy Shorts. Every animal is a friend here. But no animal is friendlier than the axolotls!

They always smile. They love what they love. And they each name themselves after their own favorite thing.

THIS IS THE STORY OF ONE AXOLOTL.
MEET...
THINKS-A-LOTL

CHAPTER 1

WELCOME TO FROWN TOWN

Thinks-a-Lotl loves to think.

He asks a lot of silly questions.

Questions like "What if an octopus wore gloves?" and "What happens if I sneeze and burp at the same time?"

While brushing his teeth one morning, Thinks-a-Lotl says to himself, "I wonder if I can frown."

"No axolotl in the history of axolotls has ever frowned," says Dad-a-Lotl from the hallway.

That does not stop Thinks from trying. He hooks his fingers to the sides of his mouth. He pulls down.

"Look! I'm frowning! I'm frowning!" shouts Thinks.

Thinks-a-Lotl takes his fingers out of his mouth. But the frown is still there.

"Huh?" says Thinks through his frowny mouth.

He pushes his cheeks up. But the frown pulls them down.

He stretches his face with both hands. He pulls back and back like a slingshot. But his mopey mouth returns as soon as he lets go.

Thinks-a-Lotl runs into the kitchen.

His family is eating breakfast.

They smile at him. Thinks frowns.

"What's the matter, son?" asks Dad.

"My face is broken!" hollers Thinks.

"I can't stop frowning!"

CHAPTER 2

TURNED UPSIDE DOWN

Thinks-a-Lotl's dad tries to calm him down on the way to school.

"Don't worry. Your face will go back to normal," says Dad-a-Lotl. "Plus, it's not like it's picture day."

"But today *is* picture day!" cries Thinks. "I'm doomed!"

Thinks goes to the back of the picture line. He needs to figure out how to turn his frown upside down. "Maybe I can trick my face into smiling," he says.

Thinks stands on his head. But his arms wobble. He bumps into a flapjack octopus named Florence.

"What are you doing, Thinks? This isn't PE class," says Florence.

Thinks-a-Lotl gets up on his feet.

"Am I smiling?" he asks.

"No," Florence replies. "I thought axolotls looked happy all the time."

Thinks explains the problem. His friend smiles and says, "I know how to help!"

Florence has strong suckers on her arms. She sticks them onto Thinks's face. Then she smooshes it all around.

"This will loosen your frowny muscles," says Florence. "I do this for my mom when her back is stiff."

Florence pulls her suckers off. *POP!*

But Thinks-a-Lotl's smile is nowhere to be found. He might be mopey forever!

CHAPTER 3

SMILES FOR MILES

"Sorry it didn't work," says Florence. She and Thinks-a-Lotl enter the library. It's set up for taking pictures. Soon it will be Thinks's turn!

"If only I could laugh," Thinks says.

"But I can't tickle myself!"

He looks around for help. Then he spots the perfect tickling machine.

It's Giddy's tail! Giddy the horseshoe crab is a Tickle Tag champ. Her tail has made many friends cry . . . with laughter!

"Excuse me, Giddy?" asks Thinks. "Would you mind tickling me?"

"Sure!" says Giddy. She starts wiggling her tail. "Tickle, tickle!"

She tickles Thinks-a-Lotl's armpits. He does not laugh.

She tickles his tummy. Nothing.

She tickles his toes. But Thinks can only frown.

"Next!" calls the fish taking pictures. Thinks sits in front of the camera.

"Okay, smile," says Mr. Blobby the blobfish.

"I can't," Thinks-a-Lotl replies. "My face is frozen in a frown."

He looks at the blobfish. "You get it. Your face is frowny too."

But then Mr. Blobby smiles bright.

"What?!" shouts Thinks. "How do you do that?"

"I just *think* of something happy!" says Mr. Blobby.

"Think?" says Thinks-a-Lotl. "I can think! I love thinking!"

He closes his eyes. He thinks a big, happy thought. There is a tickle at the corner of his mouth. His cheeks start to rise.

Thinks's smile returns, brighter than ever.

"Now *that* is a smile!" shouts Mr. Blobby. He takes Thinks-a-Lotl's picture.

CLICK!

THE REAL-LIFE CRITTERS

AXOLOTL FACTS

★ Wild axolotls are found in just one place. They live in two freshwater lakes near Mexico City, Mexico.

★ Axolotls are amphibians. Most amphibians live in water when they're young and go on land when they're adults. Not axolotls! They stay underwater their whole lives.

★ Real axolotls don't say cheese for school pictures. But their mouths do go up at the corners. It makes them look like they always have a smile on their face.

★ Feathery gills around an axolotl's face let it breathe underwater.

★ Axolotls have teeth, but they're not used for smiling. They're not for chewing either. The teeth are very tiny and used to grip things.

BLOBFISH FACTS

★ In the wild, you wouldn't find a blobfish and axolotl hanging out. Blobfish swim in the Indian, Pacific, and Atlantic Oceans.

★ Blobfish live deep, deep underwater. They stay near the ocean floor.

★ Real blobfish don't smile bright. But they aren't always frowning. This animal only looks really blobby and frowny when it is out of water. In the water, it looks like most other fish!

GLOSSARY

axolotl (AK-suh-lot-uhl)—an amphibian with four legs and webbed feet, a long tail, and gills around its face; axolotls spend their whole lives in water

calm (KAHLM)—to make someone feel less angry, worried, or excited

doomed (DOOMD)—sure to have something bad happen

frozen (FROH-zuhn)—stuck and unable to move or change

laughter (LAF-ter)—the act of smiling and making sounds with your voice because something is funny or makes you happy

mopey (MOH-pee)—sad and without energy

muscle (MUHS-uhl)—a tissue in the body that can be tightened or relaxed to make the body move

sucker (SUK-uhr)—a part on an animal's body that helps it stick to or hold on to things

DIVE DEEPER

1. What makes you happy again when you are feeling sad and mopey? Draw pictures of what makes you smile.

2. In chapter 1, Dad-a-Lotl asks Thinks what's the matter. Why do you think he asks that question?

3. What things did Thinks-a-Lotl do to try to get rid of his frown? Make a list.

4. The characters in this book are based on real animals. But the story is fiction. Flip back and point to at least three parts of the story that help you know it is fiction.

5. What are things that you can do to bring smiles to other people's faces?

ABOUT THE AUTHOR

C.W. Estes lives with his wife, two sons, one dog, and three chickens outside of Los Angeles, California. He loves reading, writing, and hearing his stories read out loud by young readers. He truly hopes that you enjoy these tales and wishes you all the best in your reading journey!

ABOUT THE ILLUSTRATOR

Irene Saluzzi grew up near the sea in Ancona, Italy, and graduated with a degree in architecture before studying entertainment design. Now, she lives in Florence and works as a freelance illustrator. She loves listening to all types of music, as well as reading novels and picture books. She looks at the world with the eyes of a child and aims to spread joy through her drawings.